THIS BOOK BELONGS TO:

_____

D1583663

For Jasper

This is a first paperback edition published in 2017.
Mr Tweed's Busy Day © Flying Eye Books 2014.

Originally published as *Mr Tweed's Good Deeds* in 2014 by Flying Eye Books,
an imprint of Nobrow Ltd. 27 Westgate Street, London E8 3RL.

Text and illustrations © Jim Stoten 2014.
Jim Stoten has asserted his right under the Copyright, Designs and Patents Act,
1988, to be identified as the Author and Illustrator of this Work.

2 4 6 8 10 9 7 5 3 1

Published in the US by Nobrow (US) Inc.
Printed in Poland on FSC® certified paper.
ISBN: 978-1-911171-22-5

Order from www.flyingeyebooks.com

WRITTEN & ILLUSTRATED BY JIM STOTEN

MR TWEED'S BUSY DAY

FLYING EYE BOOKS
LONDON — NEW YORK

The sun was shining as Mr Tweed set out on his daily walk into town. As he strolled through the park, he met Little Colin Rocodile who was looking rather glum.

"I was flying my new kite, when the string snapped!" said Colin.

"Oh my, how unfortunate," said Mr Tweed. "Let's look for it together!"

It's the perfect day for kite flying. Can you help Mr Tweed and Colin find **1** lost kite?

Feeling cheerful, Mr Tweed left the park and passed by Mrs Fluffycuddle's cottage.

"Tibbles? Timkins? Where are you both?" she called out. "Oh, Mr Tweed, I can't find my kittens! Can you help?"

"Of course!" said Mr Tweed. "They can't have gone far."

Can you spot **2** missing kittens hiding in Mrs Fluffycuddle's garden?

Mr Tweed popped into the library on his way into town. He came across Mr McMeow peering under a bookshelf.

"Is everything all right down there?" asked Mr Tweed.

"Not at all, I'm afraid my pet mice have escaped!" replied Mr McMeow.

A library is no place for **3** lost mice.
Can you help find them?

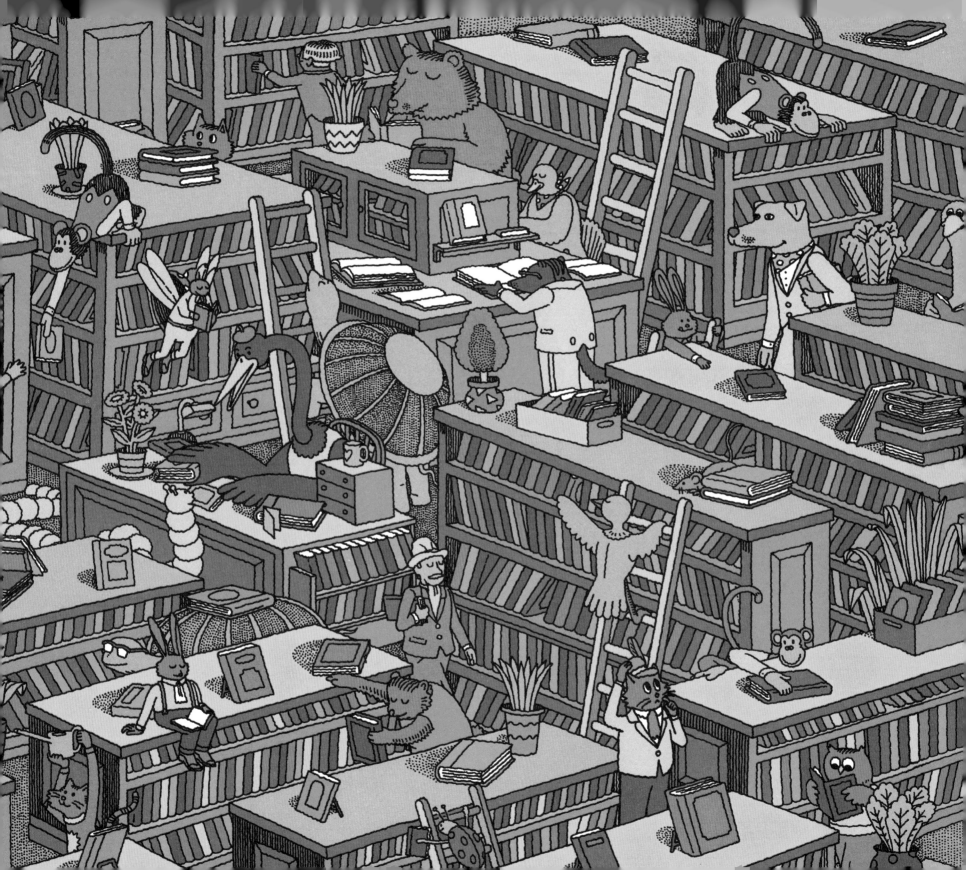

With a spring in his step, Mr Tweed reached the swimming pool. Professor Ribbet was standing by the edge looking upset.

"Oh dear, oh dear. My goldfish have jumped into the pool! Could you help me, Mr Tweed?" exclaimed Professor Ribbet.

Can you see **4** goldfish splashing around? Careful not to fall in too!

Mr Tweed walked on, feeling very happy to have helped so many people already. But what was this? Big Bear Bob was looking for something in the trees.

"Oh, hello, Mr Tweed," said Bob. "I was practising with my bow and I've lost all my arrows."

5 arrows in the woods won't be easy to find.
Can you help Mr Tweed find them?

Mr Tweed walked into a market. As he wandered through the stalls, he noticed Herman Chimps looking rather anxious.

"Good day, Mr Tweed. I had a box of pineapples but they must have rolled away!" said Herman.

"A prickly matter," said Mr Tweed. "I'd be happy to help!"

Where could **6** pineapples possibly be?
See if you can spot them in the busy crowds.

Wandering out of the market and towards the river, Mr Tweed saw Little Penny Paws crying.

"Oh, Little Penny!" Mr Tweed said. "Whatever's the matter?"

"I was carrying a bunch of flowers for my mum, but the wind caught them and they all flew into the river," she sobbed.

Look out over the busy river with Mr Tweed and Penny. Can you spot **7** floating flowers?

Mr Tweed ambled cheerfully into town, only to bump into Billy Webber, looking a little bewildered.

"Hello, Mr Tweed. I had some socks hanging on my washing line and they have all blown away somewhere…" said Billy.

Socks can't go very far without a good pair of shoes. See if you can spot **8** socks here.

As Mr Tweed turned the corner, he saw the fair was in town and Pingle Penguin came running towards him.

"I won a bunch of balloons and let them go by mistake. Do help me before they float away!" said Pingle.

The fair is filled with Ferris wheels and rollercoasters, but can you help find **9** balloons?

Mr Tweed was heading home when Pete Weasel came running up and invited him around the corner. Everyone that Mr Tweed had helped on his walk was there.

"We have thrown you a party to say thank you for all your help!" said Pete.

Hidden somewhere are **10** presents for Mr Tweed. Can you help collect them all?

"Goodbye, Mr Tweed," everyone called.

"What a great day helping people!" Mr Tweed
said, as he made his way home.

Join Mr Tweed on his second adventure... Coming soon!

MR. TWEED
AND THE BAND IN NEED
WRITTEN & ILLUSTRATED BY JIM STOTEN

FLYING EYE BOOKS

The ever-helpful Mr Tweed returns for his second search-and-find adventure, where an array of animal musicians are waiting to be found among Jim Stoten's wacky, bustling illustrations.

Order from www.flyingeyebooks.com or all good bookshops

ISBN 978-1-911171-29-4